Girls and Buoyant

Emily Crocker

First published 2017
Reprinted 2019
by Subbed In

© Emily Crocker 2019

Cover design by Dan Hogan
Book design by Sam Wieck
Text set in 8pt Domaine Text

Second edition

Printed and bound in Birraranga (Melbourne)

National Library of Australia Cataloguing-in-Publication:
Crocker, Emily
Girls and buoyant / Emily Crocker
ISBN: 9780648147527 (paperback)

Subbed In 003

www.subbed.in

These poems were written and edited on the stolen land and waterways of the Wadi Wadi people of Dharawal Country, and the Cadigal-Wangal people of the Eora Nation. This book was printed and bound on the stolen lands of the Woiwurrung (Wurundjeri) and Boon Wurrung people of the Kulin nation. Sovereignty was never ceded. Emily Crocker and Subbed In pay their respects to elders, past and present.

Always was, always will be Aboriginal land.

CONTENTS

Wool

There's not much we can do about the ocean.
She said it wearing a wool sweater. Those
carnivorous teeth curling as if a herd
of cattle would stop for her. By which
she meant; *you can't have a revolution*
without people dying.

Pinned

The sunflowers know full well they are sunflowers.
Cellophane spun with their smiles pinned back
as friends and family rumble past from
hospital reception to cock the stems
of their necks at the elevator directory.
The florist asks if they need any
help, having squeaked around
the corridors enough times. Waiting
forked-tongue behind teeth for the two young men
to say they're visiting their sister in maternity.
She'll spit out a grand symphony of
babies breath and carnations, a teddy-bear
laced down in the centre of it all.
Only eighty-dollars and she'll give you a foil
balloon for free. Was it a boy or a girl?
Too bad the sunflowers don't know
what the sun is anymore. Desperately
synthesising bleach and neon. The gold knives
of petals, too proud now for soil, lean back
in their flashy new ride. I stir sucralose
into my paper cup coffee, check the time,
and wonder what kind of boutonniere would
look best pinned to a straight-jacket.

Resolution

Look at these people. Jogging.
On January 4th. They must
hate themselves. Hate their fluorescent
sneakers made from recycled sea junk
and made by slaves. Must hate their bright
complexion as much as their white
teeth and their expensive headphones.
Must hate the sun, illuminating
their radiant taut legs flogging
into the pavement. The grinding
of cartilage. The stretch and spring of
muscles glowing out of their limbs
in heavy lumps. They must hate themselves
as I hate the morning stuck in my eye
tumbling onto the bus somehow
both hungover and employed.

Oranges

There's always an EFTPOS minimum
to be met. I won't accept the fifty-cent
fee is cheaper than anything else here.
The oranges were going for two bucks
per bag. They'd sagged by the day after;
geriatric rinds scored in the net and wept.
$10.34 at IGA was still
pending on my card. We candied them
with a peppermint teabag and rosemary you
stole from the war memorial up the road.
No-one questioned the ethics; the sugar
was already Black & Gold palm-derived
rubbish. Things have been royal since with
golden lips pouting on our oats every morning.

Plate

'Ceremony' has a dirty taste
but for the way we eat.
The ritual back and forth
of olives off your pizza.
The potatoes off my plate
when you give me too many
with all intention of
eating them yourself.
Without you here
I don't notice
the way I've eaten all the dahl
and none of the rice.
I can't reach over
with a scrag of tortilla
and steal your sauce.

Smashed

Avocado, I didn't want to settle down anyway.
A wife, two-and-a-bit kids, and a maltese terrier
called Ferret with grass stains on its arse
were never in my picture books.
Now I illustrate myself with a sneaky flatty and
that smell you can't get out of keep-cup lids
watching foxy silver women with
yellow leather gloves enter and speak.
Are those muffins gluten-free? No,
then I'll have a Bloody Mary.
Avocado, if I bought you instead
every time I needed a caffeine kick to
get me through this no annual leave
or penalty rates sandpaper drain
my digestion would be better but
I still couldn't eat my rent money.

Catalogue

Mailbox regurgitating catalogues, neighbour,
I don't know if you've boarded yourself in against
the avalanche waiting for the merchants' tables
to be thrown – or if you're just not home.
We left a candy-cane on your door handle anyway.
Best Before Nov; work was chucking them out.
Under the damp blanket of night flushed
by fairy-lights; neon-blue blaring *Happy Holidays!*
(don't shoot up in front of my garage).
We scamper to the next house with free saccharine
bubble-gum flavoured and dyed green. While a woman
watches us not touch her Mazda 4. Nylon lashes
scratching the screen door and the intermittent glow
of novelty light-up Rudolph-nose earrings warning out
as glitter lays its eggs in the carpet at her feet.
I'm sure I'll see her again on the 27th. Sheath
of receipts in hand, rote-learned returns-policy,
and a scrunched plastic bag from a different store
of shit no one wants until January sales kick in.

Nu Ro

open sunday morning silent shopping centre
inspecting plastic-bagged eyes in change
room mirrors nervous of the day believers
will soon break onto the skylights hug
the heavens so tight they leak when it rains
from up here I've heard on a good day
you can see all the way to the city it hasn't
been a good day for a while and we're not
desperate enough to sacrifice a goat yet
day is only just breaking through my skull
there isn't the body quantity here to
absorb each new flicker of alien-autopsy bulbs
scrubbing my way out of a vending
machine display window aluminium can row
rattle hand tremor lacking the grace of nature
I cannot pretend I do not belong here

Aoraki

When we ask for a map, the mouse haired woman
in a Department of Conservation fleece tells us
there's a tour where you can chip iceberg off
into your champagne flute and that the lake didn't
exist forty years ago. Then, it was a glacier.
I realise I'm waiting for a way to see the earth
not as a tourist. A fallen alien slicked in
petroleum membrane onto this bank of stones.
We walk guideless instead. The water,
blue as a raspberry Slush Puppy was
the most terrible thing I'd ever seen.

Warning signs

Headlights on in daytime
a neat red slash through '15'
to make it '21' deaths
in your lifetime.
Not including
the little black hatchback
at the start of the week.
Perhaps not either
the mother of two
in her Tarago
last Christmas.
You always think how
he tried to kill himself
beside this road.
But there are cops up and down it
every day.
And only the good
die young.

Guyra

North, through what you know as wine country
to meet you south of your days.
Granite surfaces in molars as terrain rolls
from collarbone to peach hip, lip balm
smacking through the open window.
I can't remember the names of the other rocks
since you stopped quizzing me. Moved right out
of my mind like an abattoir.

Without a half-decent coffee to be found,
a flat possum, halfway over the white line
wags its tail. Trucks rattle past. I scan
the radio for news and turn up Adele tickets
sponsored by Rick's Meats, Muswellbrook.
And drive into the oncoming collision
of eldest son's eldest sons.

The same motorcycle overtakes me every town.
Tracing each name speech therapy
they all taste like not good enough.
From a rocking-chair wedged under a door handle
Someone's paid real cash for billboards name-calling
wind farming "environmental vandalism"
and quoting Matthew, "a man shall join to his wife".

I show up with quick-sale valentines flowers
and a bottle of port, wagging my tail. Everything
looks doll-sized. The breakfast-bar stool-covers
need laundering. I am still there, sharp knees
on the countertop scratching butterfly stamps
out of raw potato halves. With my palm
between her tiny shoulder blades, fluttering
as they work away, I ask how you like us now.
You hurry me out of the kitchen,
wielding a tea towel for a champagne flute

In photos of the Lamb and Potato Festival
pumpkin relay, dolly-arms wrapping
the heavy fruit to my skinny chest,
knees stuttering underneath, I came last.
But won their hearts like a butcher's tray.
Even now I've been known to eat meat at family gatherings.
Bring out the Sunday cutlery. I'm here
for both of us to see what I am made of.
Treat each other to alcho-prep pads
at the site of incision. I quote Matthew,
"for this cause a man shall leave his father".

Paul always took the boys trout fishing
when we were up for the summer
I say how he wrapped Mary's throat
in monofilament line. You don't recall that.
I can't get the lure of T.S. Elliot out of my eye.
It's a bloody kaleidoscope of decaffeinated instant
and forbidden nail-polish remover. We're still
praying in my unborn nephew's names that
we'll build wind farms.

There are fewer broken necks in town
now everyone works in the tomato greenhouse
instead of the slaughterhouse. Who ever heard
of a liquor store gone bust? At least the pub
was built on higher ground. It smelt
like a bread-maker then and it smells like it now.

My brother loves good men.
Wins meat-raffles like a vegan.
Can tell sugar-gum from red-spotted.
Doesn't sport for introduced fish species.
He would love to inherit your pumpkin scone recipe
but eldest sons inherit farms where you're from.

You take me on a tour of all the family homes
you moved through buying a better view
of the arboretum. You know the date every one
of those trees were planted. Every one
is more beautiful than a studio in suburban Sydney.

South, I think about living out of my car.
You sent me home with cold-cut sandwiches,
and doll's furniture. These somethings fit perfectly
in the glove box. But I've been taught to fear
what it would do to the family name to
be surrounded by windows all the time.
I always admired greenhouses more than granite.

Swallows Rock

A ripped piece of foul prawn in the belly.
It didn't even taste it go down.
Mouth gasping a breathless O. Jelly-eye
greyly indignant with betrayal.
It terrified me, running up the beach
in tiny boardies, sandals flapping
yelling to my father asleep in
a straining canvas chair, t-shirt over
his plum face. The flat fish still tossing
wet sand between its joints in excruciating
futility. How ugly it would be when
you finally get a bite. The thrilling
flash of reeling it in only to find
a slippery mess all over my hands.
I picked around my veggies that evening
until the fillet was forced over my
muddy tongue. Nostrils yanked together
unable to vomit the ingratitude back up.

Pluck

In the mirrored doors, I remember
the time to plant. My father breaking
open ground. Seeds of sweat diving
from his brow as he shovelled the generous
debt afforded to him to lay his own
name in an outer corner of Sydney soil.
He filled the Corolla with free horse shit
from the side of the road and buried
lettuces, onions, beans, and carrots beneath
my hot-pink extra-small multipurpose gloves.

Today, my brother lugs a whipper snipper,
unused hedge trimmers, a barbecue gas bottle
out to the kerb while I sort decades
of swelling beer-belly Lowes polo-shirts
and polyester ties into For Charity or The Dump.
Harvesting parched pocket-sized Jim Beam
bottles from the back of the wardrobe.
Learning there must also be a time
to pluck what was planted.

Uproot

Show me the beauty amongst the shards
of loaded fathers firing wreckage into the night.
The heart-leafed philodendron thrown from its pot
lying amongst strange silvery beads of soil and
ceramic fragments dealt across the floorboards.
The plant replaced. Perhaps with chives; something useful
and easily uprooted. For the best. We've all got regrets
faced with chaos and death.

I can no longer paint the unholy up in an emperor's
mute and pervasive holiness. Time does not pass
with the quiet awe of a monk. It bustles by,
blows us down, and grumbles when we don't keep up.
The shards are a hideous danger we will
still be tasked to sweep back together. Maybe by the
hundredth occasion I will know how to repair with gold.
To a stranger, the shards will become beautiful, more holy.
To us they will be no less likely to shatter again
and more expensive when they finally do.

Southerly

Mango and coldies for dinner.
Makeshift blanket curtains
paisley and Donald Duck
illuminated over the sunroom.
The hallway door left open,
then closed, then open.
The vent grinding
its teeth out back.
Assuring my English mother
it'll start to get cool now the sun's gone down.
When the buster came
hurtling across the suburb,
windows thrown desperately
open, buttons burst
apart in revelry.
And every little hair on your arms
reaching out
to receive its cool blessing.

Fruit

The quack mistook you for a little boy.
How dreadful, said the same women
who keep laying hard-boiled
eggs in our living room. Once,
on the way to another baby shower,
I made you pull over beside the highway.
Spring and a family of ducks were trying
to cross to a golf course. At a break
in the traffic we hurried them
over, bodies craned in wide hoops.
A truckie honked at us lapping the fat
meat of his tongue to the glass, the wind
blowing up our skirts. Smog dancing like
a tinned fairy in my throat. That night,
my skull on your breastbone, our uteruses lay
back to back in begrudged silence at the
suggestion they should be in time by now.
As if they only need pool their blood and they
could buy their way out of here all on their own.

Meanwhile, Man goes on sucking apple puree
from pastel-coloured satchels and tossing
the limp plastic hulls into the ocean.
This way, there will always be new islands
to skewer with flagpoles. Duck goes on
mistaking all that glimmers for fish and
dragging up foil. We go on sewing
the buttons back on our shirts and eating
misshapen local produce so ugly
even a mother couldn't love it.

Haircuts for the apocalypse

for Clair

the first backyard haircut I got
a punishment
in the days before fancy peanut butter
snipped straight through
my hunger strike
with no better way to remind me
my place than to slash-and-burn
all the girl off me
I ate my fare in blazing silence

last time the sun tingled clipping
Canberra's buoyant sky
blades humming breathy
hungry behind your ear
you nibbled away the yesteryear
a hung bike chain around
my shoulders called it
the one-cut-wonder welling up
in pumpkin-gold marvel
at your proficiency with a pair of scissors
and volumes of generosity

Covers

Dug within the queen-sized sheets drooping overboard
our double-bed. I first thought of my hermit crab
who when I was eight buried herself under
the sawdust in one corner of her tank
and never crawled back out.
       All I had to offer was
shitty ginger-flavoured camomile tea,
half a foil of ibuprofen, and guilt-
laden reparations for greeting you this evening with
Why the fuck is the sink covered in noodles?
        My stomach thudding into your silence.
Your battery-pig recoil at the bedroom light switched on.
I dared to think we couldn't afford the ambo bill
if you sunk any deeper. My car
still sounds like a washing machine.
I reached through the stink of tea-tree and dog's ears
to coyly prise open your hand.

Pinky-promise me you won't die tonight.
You shook my little finger back.
I put the car keys on the bedside anyway
and held your cells, rocking themselves apart,
together until the pharmacy reopened.

Treatment

carcinogenic tampons
revolving-door doctors
Could you be pregnant?
the warm glow of ER
over your empty car park spew
It's perfectly normal.
morphine
ginger-wine, maca powder, fermented things
WebMD
go off the pill
everyone and their mum
the sex health specialist
4 negative gonorrhoea tests
in 12 months
Could you be pregnant?
you need an internal examination
that I won't perform
go back on the pill
you must've taken the sample
incorrectly
4 month waiting list
Where's your referral?
Call this number.
history of trauma
Are you sure?
we don't treat patients in same-sex relationships
you don't want fertility treatments
you're just in crippling pain
psychosomatic
you've run out
of bulk-billed appointments

Sum of itself

after Emily Parsons-Lord

We touch with breath
as small as a whole world and spray
ourselves back out into it.
The molecules balloon together;
stones moving through everything.
The sommelier swishes its wet weight
through the sinuses and returns with yes,
notes of cucumber and archaeology.
You comfort yourself
with cooling soda water. It bursts
on your tongue hot like political
opinion released from retreating ice shelves.
We paint the air
with talk and industry,
but think so rarely of it.
Soaked, it drools sticky down
the side of all our containers.
We pick up an empty jar and in the light,
forget immediately what we are holding.

Queenstown

I look   up   from the phone screen
having again   forgotten   the tide.
The lake's   cold   tongue.
The immense   mountains
in their prayer circle.   Blossoming
in tectonic   pride.   Never
reaching   for the   sky's crisp
pretence   of forever   but
leading   with the head,   always.

Brunch

The air is trying to hold itself up, chin high,
against the humidity as the leaves refuse to fall on time.
We match its grief by sleeping in. Flooding
the place out with snore-spluttered drool and waking
up with bacon sizzling under our tongues.
Need to soak up all the maple. Bread and surfaces.
Your knife could've dug clean through
your grandmother's porcelain. As if
you were descended from a coal mining dynasty.
As if there were any of us who weren't unearthed
in gold blood and sausage chains of guts
to a coal mining dynasty. Now we can't stop
poking our penises down rabbit warrens straight
into the smouldering earth, weeping mute smoke
like it forgot it should've rained by now
in all the small talk about socks and sandals
for fall season fashion and how pretty the trees aren't.

Illawarra

The road runs a smooth
palm over and around
shaping the escarpment.

Wets its lips
with a light tongue tip tracing up
the lush littoral forest.

We curl in each bend.
Push a massaging tyre-tread heel
into the slopes and dives.

It's just enough
for us to keep our hands off each other
while you drive.

Lawns

You only come home to dig graves now
all your childhood pets are dying. You think of them
sometimes when it rains and an old squeaky chew toy
is retrieved from the bottom of the garden.
The grass seeds sprouting in the seams of dog's teeth,
a ragged towel coffin two feet below the lavender.

When your grandmother was your age she buried
a still-born loaf of bread clothed in a lavender
print tea-cloth so her husband wouldn't know she'd spoiled
the flour. The premature dough proofed anyway.
From two feet below the soil a black-eye blossomed
silent until the glutinous monster broke into daylight.

When you were born your father bought a Subaru
on finance because he wasn't in debt enough yet
to be granted a mortgage. He chanted this story
like the only reason you were sent into the garden
to pick which apple stick you'd like to get flogged with
and retrieve it clenched between your teeth was because

he promised himself it'll be the greenest lawn
on the whole damn street. Pissed on it every day
through ten years of drought. Until the neighbours
sent the cops around. To show them, he cemented it
over and put in a salt-water swimming pool. Now he has
no lawn and all his childhood friends are dying.

He thinks of them sometimes when daylight beats
through the silence. There are too many empty beer coasters
on the back-patio card table overlooking the pool.
For now, you count up the slices and bury the funeral loaves
to avoid the payday bank queues. You hope bread
will grow on trees if only you indebt yourself to the ground.

Gaps

Vacuum sucked together
gaps emerge between flesh curves.
New holes blossoming open
as we roll into the awaiting space.
The white noise of my dust
blown through your light
echoing between my forearms.

Your lumpy sternum.
My lumpy forehead. The slots
between my lanky toes
seized by chunky joints that can't quite
stretch far enough to accommodate
yours between them.

The days between Sunday and Tuesday
and Wednesday and Friday.
The nights.
The darkness fallen over the triangle
that travels between us
and refuses to be simple nothingness
to pass silently through.

The space assumed by the black
that swallows whole the longing pebbles
skipped out into it and burps
the clean mineral aftertaste
back in my face.

The spectrum of jagged warping sounds
that would come streaming out
if we could refract its solid
censoring cloak. Slices of tones

split from the air that vibrates
so confidently it solidifies into
a grainy quiet concrete mould
of the distance.

The blank
that would remain below it.
You make me conscious of the void
and how blessedly we inhabit it.

AUTHOR ACKNOWLEDGEMENTS
Thanks to the Enough Said crew in Wollongong
for being my first poetry home. Especially to Lorin
Elizabeth, my original poetry godmother, for your
constant encouragement. I am grateful to everyone
I've had a meal or a conversation with in the past year.
Particularly Will, Jen and Dan, my beloved friends
known as 'The Avos', Jay, and Paige. Thanks also to
Stacey, Dan, and Rory for all your work creating this
chapbook with me.

ABOUT THE AUTHOR
Emily Crocker writes and performs poetry. You
might have seen her at BAD!SLAM!, Noted Festival,
Unspoken Words, or Word in Hand. Emily can also be
found at Enough Said Poetry Slam in Wollongong or
studying at the University of Wollongong.

'Covers' was originally published in *Ugly Pineapple*.
November 2016. Print.

Subbed In is a not-for-profit DIY literary organisation and small press based in Sydney, Australia. Subbed In's program of publications and events aim to elevate the voices of trans people, people of colour, non-binary people, sex workers, women, people with a disability, LGBTQIA+ people, First Nations people, survivors, working class people, and anyone who finds themselves on the margins of the supremely white, cis, heteronormative, capitalist, colonial, ableist, patriarchal hellscape in which we live.

For more information visit: *www.subbed.in*